LITTLE BO PEEP

BY KEELY CHACE ILLUSTRATED BY NICOLA ANDERSON

Little Bo Peep sat watching her sheep
in a pasture by a lake.
If only Bo Peep hadn't *counted* the sheep,
then she might have stayed awake!

The sheep saw her doze, so they tickled her nose,
and they nudged her floppy hand.
Bo Peep didn't stir—there was no waking her.
Things were going just as planned!

So off to the park went the sheep on a lark,
and they tried each thrilling thing.
They slid down the slide, took a sailboat ride,
and found they **LOVED** to swing!

The sheep did all right at flying kites,
and they dazzled at croquet.
They played some ball. They enjoyed it all!
They were having quite a day!

And still, the sheep didn't see Bo Peep,
so they picnicked on some grass.
After they ate, they just couldn't wait
to join in a yoga class!

Meanwhile, Bo woke and groaned, "Oh, no,"
when she found her flock all gone.
"Well, OK, sheep, you want hide-and-seek?
Here I come! The game is ON!"

So Little Bo Peep followed tracks of sheep
to the park and she could tell
that her flock was near . . . they were somewhere here!
She knew by the sheepy smell.

A determined Bo looked high and low
into every hiding place—
under trees and flowers, and it felt like hours,
but she couldn't find a trace.

She looked in the grass, through the yoga class:
there were no sheep hiding there.
She checked by the swings, didn't find a thing.
Had they vanished into thin air?

And then at last, Little Bo ran fast
to the pond and spied a boat.
Instead of sails, it had fleecy tails—
something Bo couldn't help but note.

Little Bo Peep had found her sheep!
And she said, "You're all OK!
Well, my friends, you got me again.
Seems I lose you every day!"

"Now it's time to go!" said Little Bo
to her flock so wild and woolly.
And I'm glad to say, on that sleepy day,
she learned her lesson fully:

Watch like a hawk with a tricky flock,
and keep your wits about you.
Don't count sheep, or you'll fall asleep,
and they'll all go play without you!

If you enjoyed these itty bittys
and the story that they told,
then we would love to hear from you,
our readers young and old!

Please send your comments to:
Hallmark Book Feedback
P.O. Box 419034
Mail Drop 100
Kansas City, MO 64141

Or e-mail us at:
booknotes@hallmark.com